The Patchwork parrot
dresses up

by A J Wood
Illustrated by Juliette Clarke

PRICE
STERN
SLOAN

PRICE STERN SLOAN LIMITED, NORTHAMPTON, ENGLAND

"What shall we do today?" said Patchwork Parrot,
wriggling out from the end of the bed.
No one answered.

"Shall we play ball?" he asked Big Bear.
Big Bear didn't answer. Big Bear was asleep.

"Shall we play I-spy?" he asked Tommy Train.
Tommy Train didn't answer. Tommy Train couldn't talk.

"Shall we play hide-and-seek?"
Patchwork Parrot asked Lucy Doll.
Lucy Doll sniffed and sighed. She didn't play
with parrots.

"I wish Billy was here,"
said Patchwork Parrot to
himself.
But Billy was at school.

"Bother these toys!" said Patchwork Parrot
in his extra-special-grumpy voice.
"I shall find something exciting to do, all by myself!"

Patchwork Parrot looked
at himself in the mirror.

He didn't like what he saw.

Once he had been a smart
red parrot with green
wings and a stripy tail.

That was years ago.

Now he was a scruffy
red parrot with patches
on his tummy and
his tail.

"Bother these patches!" said Patchwork Parrot
in his ever-so-cross voice.
"I wish I could cover them up."

Then Patchwork Parrot had an idea.

"I know!" he said. "Today I shall dress up.
I shall wear a shirt and a coat and a scarf.
I shall wear boots on my feet and a hat on my
head, just like Billy. Then I'll be the smartest
parrot in this house!"

Big Bear opened one sleepy eye.

"That won't be difficult," he said.
"You're the only parrot here!"

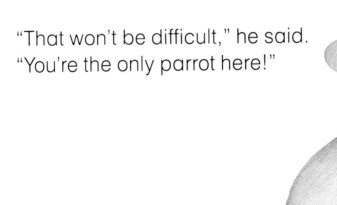

Patchwork Parrot pretended not to hear.

"Bother that bear!"
he muttered under his breath.

Then he marched across the carpet to the
wardrobe where Billy kept his clothes.

Click!

Carefully he opened
the door. Inside were
lots of exciting things
to dress up in.

"Hurray!"
said Patchwork
Parrot.

There were hats and scarves, shirts and jumpers,
jackets and coats, and socks and boots, and shoes.

First of all, Patchwork Parrot tried on a clean white shirt.
But he couldn't work out where to put his wings.

"Bother this shirt!" said Patchwork Parrot.
And he trod on the
sleeve by mistake
and left a dirty mark.

Then he tried on a smart red jacket.
It was too big and he couldn't do the buttons up.

"Bother these buttons!" he said,
as one fell off and
rolled across the
carpet.

Next, he pulled out a neat blue hat
that Billy wore to go fishing.
But it kept slipping down over his head
so he couldn't see where he was going.

"Bother this hat!" said Patchwork Parrot
as he walked into a chair leg.

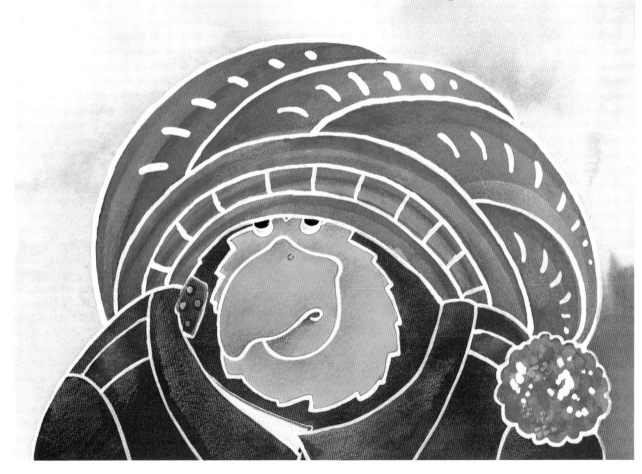

Last of all, he tried on a pair of Billy's shoes.
They were black and shiny with long green laces.

And they were much too large
for Patchwork Parrot.
But he put them on anyway.

He'd seen Billy tying up
the laces into neat bows.
But he couldn't remember
how to do it himself.

"That'll do!" said
Patchwork Parrot,
tying the laces together
into a big knot.

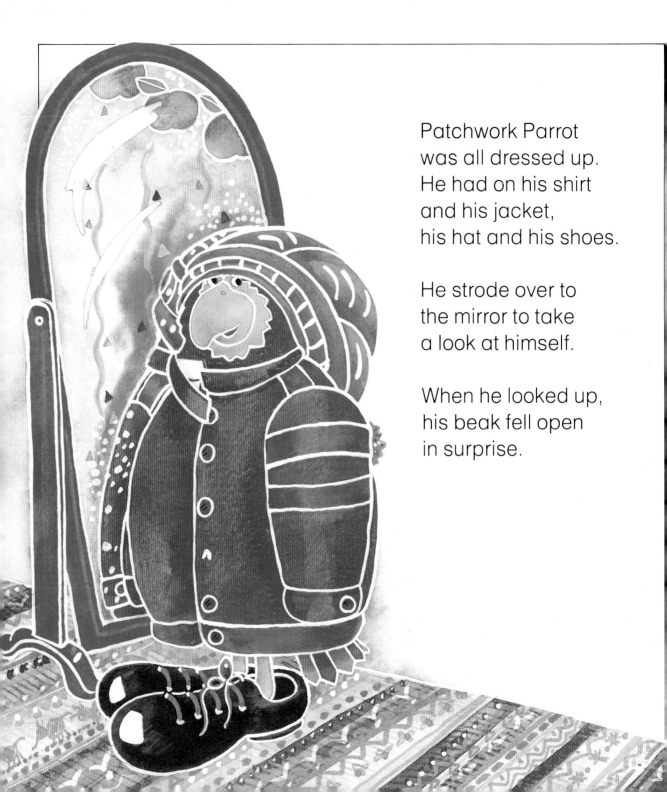

Patchwork Parrot
was all dressed up.
He had on his shirt
and his jacket,
his hat and his shoes.

He strode over to
the mirror to take
a look at himself.

When he looked up,
his beak fell open
in surprise.

He didn't look smart at all. In fact, he looked STUPID!

"Bother these clothes!" said Patchwork Parrot,
putting them all back in the wardrobe.
"My patches look a million times smarter!"

"No, they don't!" growled Big Bear.
"Yes, they do!" scowled Patchwork Parrot.

But he didn't think they did really.
So he shuffled off into the corner
feeling sad.

Just then Billy came home.
He raced up the stairs and
looked round the room.

"Come on Patchwork Parrot!"
he yelled, spotting him in
the corner.

"We're going out!
Jimmy Jones brought a real
parrot to school today.
But I told him not even a real
parrot is as smart as you."

"Let's go and show him!"

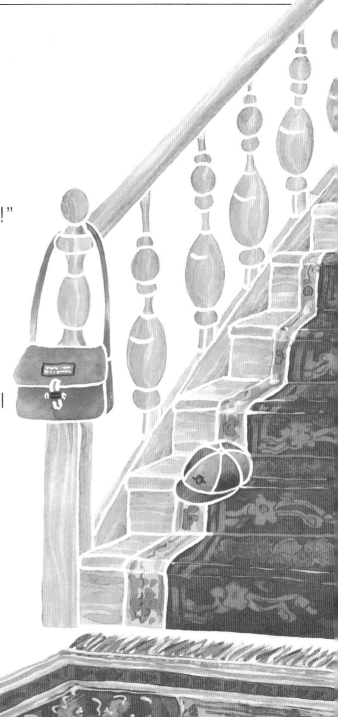

Patchwork Parrot puffed
out his chest with pride.
He looked down at the patches
on his tummy and his tail.

"Who needs clothes?"
he said to Big Bear as he
disappeared out of the door.